Welcome to Mixed Up Land

Mixed Up Land's like a place that's real
With mixed up friends you can almost feel
You can only get there when you're fast asleep
Past the river so wide, through the jungle deep
Near the grassland, lake and the mountains high
And the caves and the swamp and the desert so dry.

So close your eyes and drift away
To the place where the mixed up animals play
They're colourful and kind and they understand
That they're happy and safe in Mixed Up Land
With their mixed up bodies and heads and feet
They're the silliest friends that you ever will meet

When playtime's over in Mixed Up Land
The mixed up animals understand
That you'll wake up at home in your nice warm bed
In the place where you lay while this story was read
So don't feel sad when this story ends
'Cause you're never too far from your mixed up friends

Orderly Oscar

"Someone stole my oranges, I don't know who
I must try and find them. Tell me, was it you?"

One lovely morning in Mixed Up Land
The sun rose over the desert sand
Far beyond the mountains three
Grew Orderly Oscar's favourite tree

As he opens his eyes and then stretches his wings
Oscar wakes up and then, yawning, he sings,
"From the top of my head to the toes on my feet
I'm ever so hungry - is it time to eat?"

He leapt from his nest and flew to the ground
By the large heavy rock that was purple and round
To the stack of banana leaves piled up so high
Hiding his oranges from all who passed by

He scattered the leaves so shiny and green
But not one single orange could even be seen
Orderly Oscar then started to cry,
"Someone stole my oranges, I can't think why!"

Brilliant Betty was wriggling around
In her kitchen located just under the ground
Her window was open and facing the sky
And through it she heard her friend Oscar's loud cry

"Oh, Oscar, my good friend, what's happened to you"
Asked Betty who always knew just what to do
"Someone stole my oranges, I don't know who
I must try and find them. Tell me, was it you?"

Brilliant Betty shook her starfish head
"I do not take things that are not mine", she said
"I'll help you to look for them, so don't be sad
I'm sure that we'll find them before they turn bad"

Betty and Oscar set off down the track
To try and get some of the oranges back
They went to the fish pond to ask Friendly Frank
If he knew who was guilty of this nasty prank

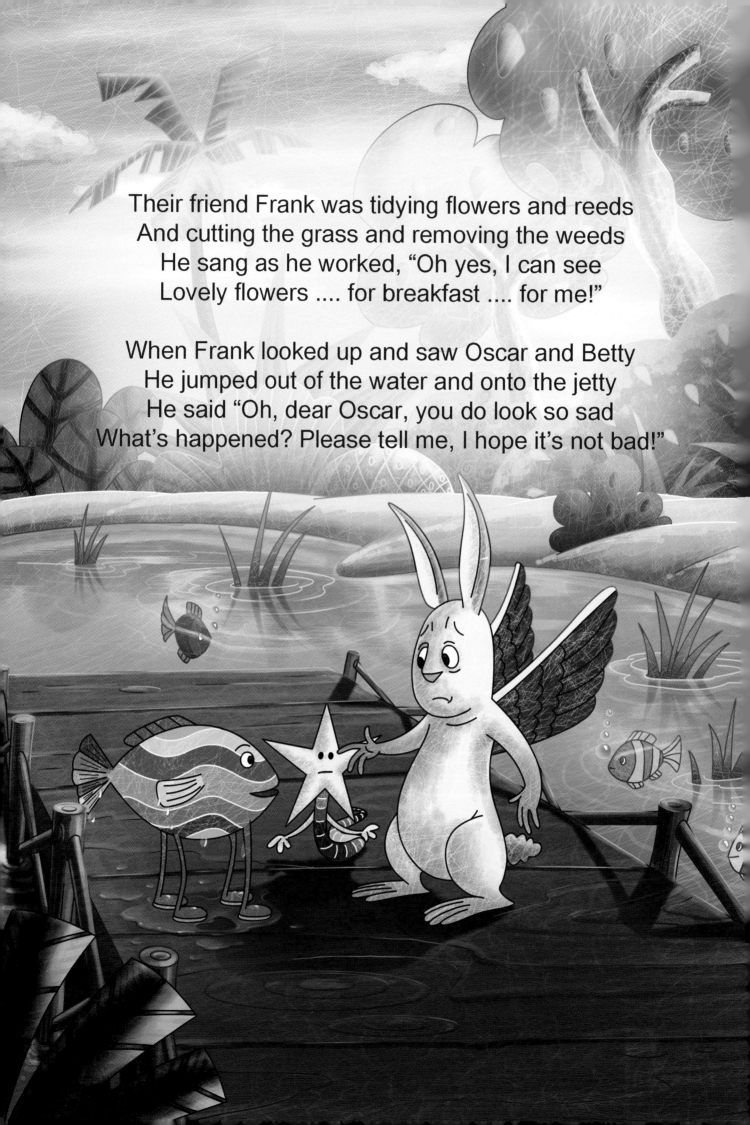

Their friend Frank was tidying flowers and reeds
And cutting the grass and removing the weeds
He sang as he worked, "Oh yes, I can see
Lovely flowers .... for breakfast .... for me!"

When Frank looked up and saw Oscar and Betty
He jumped out of the water and onto the jetty
He said "Oh, dear Oscar, you do look so sad
What's happened? Please tell me, I hope it's not bad!"

Oscar told Frank of his nasty surprise
And he said, "You can check with your very own eyes
Someone stole my oranges, I don't know who
I must try and find them. Tell me, was it you?"

Frank was so friendly he kindly replied,
"My dear Oscar, be sure I would never have tried
To take oranges, flowers or such property
If I knew that the items were not mine, you see"

Brilliant Betty and Oscar and Frank
Wanted to find who committed this prank
"We'll help you to look for them, so don't be sad
We're sure that we'll find them before they turn bad"

The three friends agreed they'd keep searching all day
And so they continued to go on their way
"We must ask some more friends but who shall we pick?"
And then they arrived at the jungle so thick

Deep in the jungle in a clearing so wide
"There's Woolly William", Friendly Frank cried
"Whenever I come here it's always the same
William is playing his coconut game"

Spinning them high and spinning them low
Spinning them fast and spinning them slow
Everywhere coconuts flying about
But then William stopped when he heard Oscar shout

Oscar told William about his surprise
And said, "You can check with your very own eyes
Someone stole my oranges, I don't know who
I must try and find them. Tell me, was it you?"

William looked straight into Oscar's sad eyes
And said, "Oscar, my friend, you must realise,
I would never take so much as even a pea
If I knew it belonged to another, not me"

William continued to tell his friends three
That stealing is something to take seriously
To find out who did it I'm sure you'll agree
That Queen Mary's the one who you really must see.

The mixed up animals all understand
That Queen Mary's the wisest in all Mixed Up Land
She lives in her palace so close to the sky
Past the desert and swamplands up mountains so high

The four friends decided that they'd have to call
On the help of Queen Mary, the wisest of all
Each friend they encountered as they made their way
Was told of the oranges stolen that day

They saw Lazy Lenny in the swamp soft and green

By the dry sandy desert Silly Sarah was seen

In the lush fertile grassland they met Dozey Dave

And young Nervous Nigel at the front of his cave

Each Friend that they met had told them that they'd known
It was wrong to take something that was not your own
They offered to help because Oscar was sad
And they hoped they'd find his fruit before it turned bad

When they got to the mountain past the swamp soft and green
They climbed up to the palace of Mary the Queen
The four friends explained to the good queen that day
How the fruit had been stolen and taken away

The friends thank Queen Mary and bow down quite low
Then back down the mountain to the valley they go
Past the caves and the pond with its water so clean
To the place by the creek as described by the queen

When they get there they stare in complete disbelief
When they see the identity of the fruit thief
One of their friends, Snappy Susan's her name,
Is standing there bowing her head down in shame

Oscar told Susan about his surprise
And said, "Now I see with my very own eyes
Someone stole my fruit and I didn't know who
But now I am sure of the thief and it's you!"

"I did take your oranges" Susan replied
"And it would be much worse if I hid them and lied
I took them last night, I was feeling quite sad
And I thought that it might help me not feel so bad"

Susan looked up as her friends stood around
And big tear drops fell from her eyes to the ground
She knew what she'd done was quite wrong and she cried,
"I stole them and it makes me feel bad inside!"

But then Frank and Betty and Oscar and friends
Said, "We will forgive you if your stealing ends"
"It will", promised Susan, "from this very day
I've now learned my lesson I'm happy to say"

The mixed up friends looked at each other and smiled
Susan had been like a naughty young child
Stealing is naughty and stealing is bad
Stealing makes everyone feel very sad

Susan returned all the fruit to her friend
And Oscar's distress had now come to an end
He said, "I'm still hungry, let's all have some food"
And the friends all agreed they were just in the mood

They sent out a message across Mixed Up Land
That the very same day a big party was planned
With nice things to eat and to drink and a band
That played music to dance to 'till no one could stand!

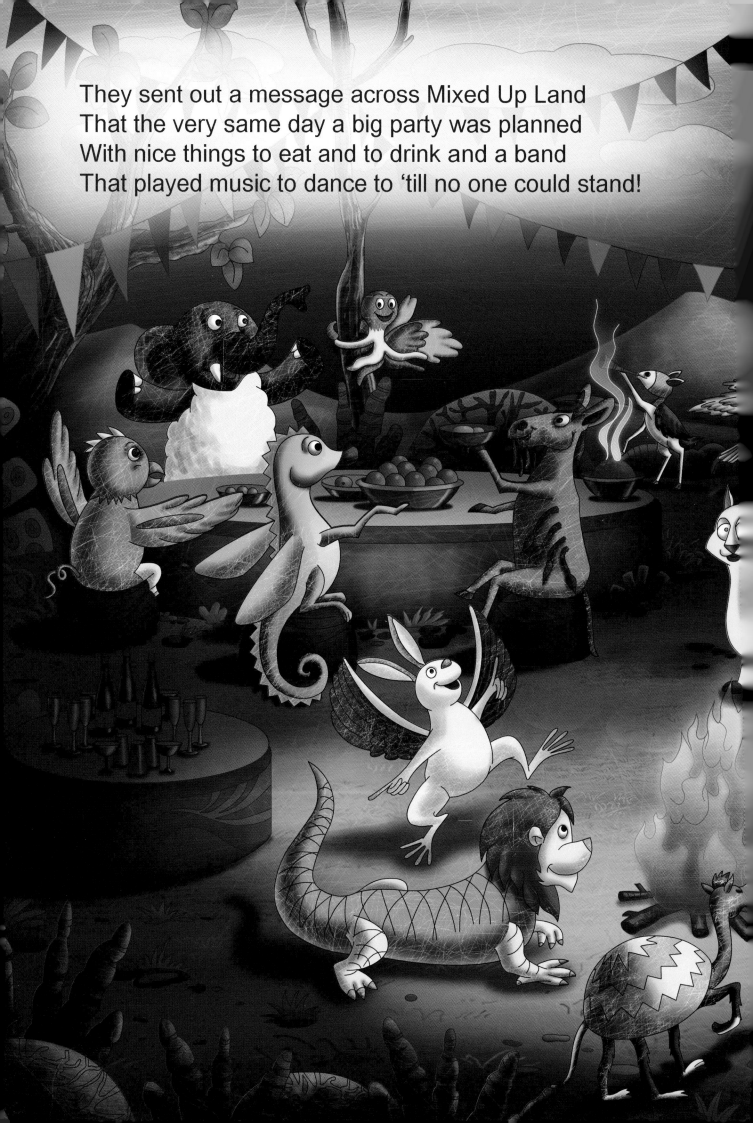